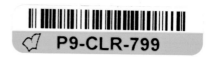

For my mother and father —F.B.
For Emily and Larry Koltnow with lots of love! —L.N.

If You Give a Pig a Party

If You Give a Pig a Party

BY Laura Numeroff

ILLUSTRATED BY Felicia Bond

SCHOLASTIC INC.
New York Toronto London Auckland
Sydney Mexico City New Delhi Hong Kong

ISBN-13: 978-0-545-21530-5
ISBN-10: 0-545-21530-7

Text copyright © 2005 by Laura Numeroff.
Illustrations copyright © 2005 by Felicia Bond.
All rights reserved. Published by Scholastic Inc., 557 Broadway, New York, NY 10012, by arrangement with HarperCollins Children's Books, a division of HarperCollins Publishers. SCHOLASTIC and associated logos are trademarks and/or registered trademarks of Scholastic Inc.

12 11 10 9 8 7 6 5 4 3 2 1 9 10 11 12 13 14/0

Printed in Mexico 49

First Scholastic printing, September 2009

is a registered trademark of HarperCollins Publishers

If you give a pig a party,

she's going to ask for some balloons.

When you give her the balloons,
she'll want to decorate the house.

When she's finished,
she'll put on her favorite dress.

Then she'll call all her friends
to invite them to the party.

Her friends won't be home,
so you'll go with her to look for them.

On the way, she'll see a street fair.

She'll want you to take her
on the bumper cars.

All her friends will be there.

Then you'll have to
take her on all the rides.

She'll want to play all the games, too.

When she's done, she'll ask you for some ice cream.

When she's finished eating the ice cream,
she'll need to change her clothes.
You'll have to take her home.

She'll ask her friends
to come along.

On the way, she'll start a game of hide-and-seek.

When you finally get home, you'll have to make dinner.

Then she'll want to have a sleepover.
You'll have to find pajamas

and blankets and pillows for everyone.

When she sees the pillows, she'll probably start a

pillow fight.

Then she'll make a
fortress out of blankets.

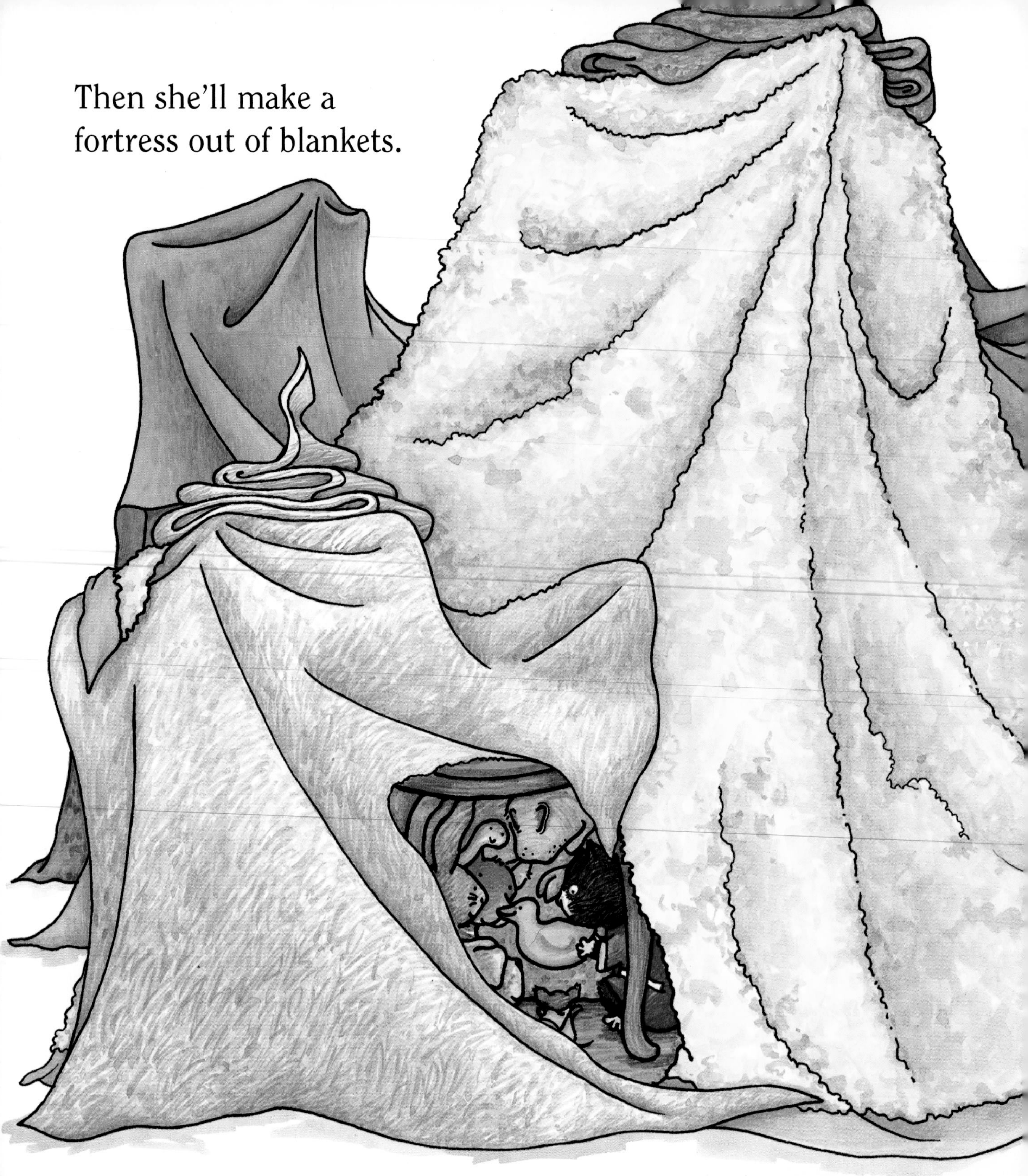

Of course, when she's finished,
she'll want to decorate it.
So she'll ask for some

balloons.

And chances are,

if you give her some balloons,

she's going to ask you
for a party.